For Amanda, Hannah, Dylan,
Ceri and Kate
J.S.

ISBN: 0-307-17521-9   A MCMXCV

Printed and bound in China.

First published in Great Britain in 1995 by Reed Consumer Books Limited.

Library of Congress Cataloging-in-Publications Data:

Shipton, Jonathan.
No biting, horrible crocodile! / Jonathan Shipton; illustrated by Claudio Muñoz.
p.   cm.
"An Artists & Writers Guild book."
Summary: Flora acts like a horrible crocodile, biting all the other children in school,
until one day she goes too far.
[1. Behavior--Fiction. 2. Bullies--Fiction. 3. Schools--Fiction.] I. Muñoz, Claudio, ill. II. Title.
PZ7.S5576No   1995
[E]--dc20   94-43817
CIP   AC

NO BITING, Horrible Crocodile!

Written by **Jonathan Shipton**

Illustrated by **Claudio Muñoz**

ARTISTS & WRITERS GUILD BOOKS
Golden Books®
Western Publishing Company, Inc.

This is me
and Mom
and Monkey
going to school.

This is Miss Jane.
This is where I sit.

And this is Steven!

We like our new school.
And we like Miss Jane.
But what we can't stand,
what spoils everything,
is . . .

FLORA!

Flora bites!
She's a Horrible Crocodile
and she follows us everywhere!
All the time!
Even if we hide.

Even if we say,

"Go away, FLORA!
We don't like
Horrible Crocodiles!"

She still gets us.
She creeps up from behind
and she

SNAPS!

Miss Jane says we can't snap back because biting is wrong for everyone.
(Even Steven.)

But Flora doesn't care
because she's a crocodile
and crocodiles
DON'T CARE!

One day
the Horrible Crocodile
makes a Horrible Crocodile mistake . . .

She makes Monkey

*sc**REAM***

at the top of his lungs!
It is so loud
that Flora jumps
right out of her crocodile skin!

All the clay turns to rock,
  all the babies jump in their carriages,
  the traffic skids to a stop,
    the little old ladies drop their bags,
    and their hats fall off.

And Flora decides
she doesn't want to be a crocodile
anymore.

She is very, very sorry
about Monkey's arm.

So we make him
a hospital bed.

Now he's feeling better.
And so is Flora.

And she's never going to bite anybody . . .

. . . ever again!